When reading through this story book
Just set your mind quite free
And join us in another world:
The world of fantasy.

Returning to those balmy days
When you were very small,
Then you believed in everything
And heard adventure's call.

No one has reached the rainbow's end
And found that wealth of gold
But fairies know if it exists –
Or so we have been told.

Now join us at the rainbow's start
For a story that's quite true,
Of a wand and fairy, made of gold,
Inlaid with diamonds too.

Although they're many miles apart,
When one you do discover,
Inside you'll find the Wizard's map
Which directs you to the other.

There is a final secret
Which we dare not tell you here;
When you have found the Wizard's map
All will become quite clear.

Fantasy Publications Ltd
14 Windsor Road
Douglas
ISLE OF MAN

© Printed in England by
Perivan Colour Print
Williams Lea Group

UK Representation
Fantasy Publications Ltd
Europe House
World Trade Centre
London E1 9AA

Long, long ago, in the days of mystery and great adventure, a strange sound came forth from a forest glade; a sound heard by no mortal being and only the animals of the forest gathered in wonder, at the place where a strange little creature lay born.

One of the animals, older and wiser than the rest, told them that they had missed a wonderful sight and, had they arrived earlier, they might have seen the birth of one who may be the very last fairy; also, they would have learned a great secret that has never been revealed. But alas! All that remained of the mother was a tiny pile of golden dust which lit up the night, as it did in the primeval forests of long ago and which can be seen, even today, in pieces of coal.

The forest animals, realising that she might well be a princess, were all agreed that it was up to them to care for this tiny mite whom they decided to call 'Devonia'. Gently, they lifted her up and laid her in a discarded shoe.

Just then The Wise One saw something atop the golden pile. He picked it up, saw that it was a tiny crown, and immediately flew off to take this treasure to his Master.

All night The Wise One flew, for his Master's home was at least two days' travel on foot and, by the time he reached it, it was well into daylight hours.

For three, long years, The Wise One had been searching for treasure to please his Master, the Wonderful Wizard Kitwillie and, although he had failed to find it, he knew that his Master would be well pleased with what he held firmly in his beak. He flopped onto the sill, almost exhausted, hopped through his special hole and onto his perch. At first his Master did not notice him as he was busy writing down the spell for his magic bubble; inside ranted and raved a particularly naughty goblin who had terrorised the neighbourhood for a long time. The old man, whose memory was becoming a bit feeble, wrote all his new spells in a big book lest he forgot them. It went like this:

Round and round inside you'll run,
Because it's empty, you'll have no fun.
Although it's only made from rain,
You can't get out – you'll try in vain.

Kitwillie was really a kind old man and would keep the goblin locked up only until he had learned his lesson. On hearing a sound behind him, Kitwillie turned around and was overjoyed to see his friend whom he had rescued from the Wicked Witch Hazel many years before. He had also taken her broomstick to keep her out of mischief. On hearing his friend's story and examining the tiny treasure, the Wizard was almost overcome with grief when he realised that this, indeed, might portend the last fairy: a baby, alone in some strange forest. He trembled when The Wise One told him that he had been flying from the west which was the direction of Witch Hazel's domain. For a few seconds Kitwillie was silent, for he had known Devonia's mother very well. Suddenly, he leapt to his feet and, without further ado, gathered everything needed for a long journey and prepared to set off in search of Devonia.

hen The Wise One, whose name, incidentally, was Jacko, was rested, he and his Master set off towards the distant forest. For certain reasons to do with the treasure for which Jacko was searching, we were going to keep his name secret but, as no other name seems to fit, let us hope that nobody will mind too much. In his haste, poor old Kitwillie fell straight over the first stile he came to and was only too glad to slow down when his friend told him to.

On the night of Devonia's birth, none of the animals had noticed the black bat flying back and forth through the trees and, although he could not see anything, he overheard every word that had been spoken by Jacko and, by the time daylight came, he was hanging upside down in the old archway beneath the ruined castle which was Witch Hazel's lair. Within twenty-five squeaks she had the whole story. She ranted and cursed the Fairy Queen who had been her worst enemy for many years. Now she had to contend with another whose powers, in time, would exceed her own. She also cursed the Wizard who had stolen her magic broomstick; since that day her crotchety back and knees had become worse from having to walk everywhere; however, she decided that once and for all she must rid herself of this menace and, within a few hours, she was nearing the birthplace. The woodland animals who by now all knew of Devonia's birth, were quick to realise the danger and, although most of them fled when Witch Hazel entered the clearing, one daring squirrel snatched Devonia from her sleeping place, scuttled up a tree, and popped her into a knot-hole where she immediately fell asleep beside a dormouse.

Witch Hazel's rage was uncontrollable and she tied herself in knots, jumping up and down, cursing the squirrel, her crotchety knees and the loss of her broomstick which would have enabled her to reach Devonia. Just then, she spied a woodcutter who was searching for just the right timber for the building of a fine ship. She put her spells to work and, within a few seconds, the woods echoed to the sound of his saw. When the tree began to tremble so did everything living inside. The spider (who had just made Devonia an everlasting dress) and the woodworm ran for their lives. The little worm fell into a hole and plunged down and down to the bottom of the tree. Devonia and the dormouse never heard a sound and slept peacefully on.

Alas! There was no sign of Devonia when, next day, the Wizard arrived on the scene. Jacko immediately showed him to the shoe which stood completely empty and a deathly silence pervaded the clearing. All the animals had fled from the wrath of Witch Hazel. Poor Kitwillie sat on the tree stump, holding his head in his hands in utter despair and wondering what he should do when, right behind him, a very dazed and dusty woodworm came crawling out of the hole in the tree trunk. Now, with all the rush and excitement of the last two days, Jacko had hardly had time to eat anything and, when he saw this plump little morsel, his eyes lit up. Jacko was just about to devour poor Woody when he heard a tiny squeak that sounded like, "wait". Jacko was taken aback for he had never heard a woodworm speak before and he quickly took a step backwards. Woody promised that in exchange for his life he would tell Jacko everything he knew about Devonia, the squirrel and the woodcutter.

Witch Hazel had fully expected the arrival of her old enemy Kitwillie and, although she had made herself invisible, she was silly enough to hide behind a bush. All the while she had been laughing and cackling to herself at the Wizard's distress but, when she realised that the little maggot was giving everything away, she almost flew without her broomstick and had to rush off into the forest where the Wizard could not hear her rantings which went like this:

Round and round and up and down
I'll rave and shout and scream.
I'll put a curse upon this place
That *will* dry up the stream.

As soon as Jacko told Kitwillie the message of the little woodworm, the old Wizard brightened up and set off immediately to find the felled tree. As Witch Hazel saw him disappearing in the opposite direction from where he lived, a crafty grin cracked her old face. She would go to his castle and regain her broomstick; perhaps, then, she would be able to follow the trail of both her old enemies. As soon as it was dark she summoned the forty strongest bats in the forest for she would need them to carry the broomstick from Kitwillie's window. When all was ready she set off for the Wizard's castle.

For a long time Kitwillie searched all the places he could think of where ships were built; then, one day, Jacko made an amazing discovery while he was talking to a woodpecker. Apparently, on returning to his nest, the poor woodpecker had found that the tree and the only egg had disappeared. After a long search he found the town to which the tree had been taken only to find that the egg had rolled out of the hole and had broken on the cobbles of the shipyard. The woodpecker told Jacko the town, the name of the ship that had been built from his home and he wished him the best of luck with his quest. Kitwillie was overjoyed at this news. He reached the town amid great rejoicing for the very ship was sailing that day. Kitwillie rushed down to the shore. Too late! In sad silence he watched the ship sailing out to sea. He reached for his magic wand of immense power so that he could transport himself onto the ship. Alas! It had gone! During his travels he had lost the one treasure which constituted most of his power. In desperation he bade Jacko follow the ship wherever it may sail and said that he would, somehow, follow later. Kitwillie was in real trouble. Let's see if we can help him solve his problem.

He's lost the power he used to have,
He's lost the magic words
That helped him rise up in the sky
Like all the soaring birds.
To reach the ship he has no chance,
He's really in dismay;
Now find the spell to do the trick
And send him on his way.

After many weary hours of fruitless thought, Kitwillie saw the ship disappearing over the horizon with a tiny black cloud right behind it. Suddenly, he realised what it was. He had seen it before. Witch Hazel, after two years, had managed to regain her broomstick. By sheer chance she had arrived there at exactly the same time as Kitwillie. In desperation, the Wizard called on all his friends of the deep and, within a short time, had all the help he needed plus a few simple items found scattered on the shore.

Kitwillie decided that it would be far better to travel beneath the waves where everything was serene and calm and, remembering the spell for his magic bubble, a perfect carriage was soon formed. With the help of two friendly dolphins, he set off into an amazing submarine world and felt humbled by what he saw.

The dolphins had already heard of Devonia's plight for the language of the animals travels at amazing speed and had reached the shores of far-distant lands; indeed, it was causing a great fuss throughout the entire animal kingdom, from mighty elephant to tiny mouse. The dolphins strained at their harness in their endeavour to catch up with the ship which was driven ever onwards by the wind; aboard, was the cargo of adventurers seeking a new world.

Meanwhile, old Witch Hazel was having the time of her life for she had never thought that she would fly again.

She looped the loop
And did a swoop
And then a twist and turn
And then at last
She went so fast
The twigs began to burn.

She giggled to herself hysterically, thinking of old Kitwillie left stranded on the shore. She had deliberately made him lose his wand with one of her wicked spells. Just as Witch Hazel was doing her final swoop she saw something beneath the waves and she almost plunged into the sea with amazement. Her eyes bulged and, in her rage, she almost bit a piece out of her broomstick. There, serenely beneath the water, sailed none other than her enemy.

Witch Hazel cursed and tried every spell she could think of to burst Kitwillie's magic bubble but all to no avail. The water protected him perfectly and, unaware, he sailed peacefully onwards.

Meanwhile, way ahead in the brave little ship, poor Devonia didn't feel well at all; neither did the little dormouse for that matter. When they had awoken, they had found themselves completely trapped in their tiny hiding place by a thick black substance and, for what seemed like an eternity, all they could hear was the banging and shouting of humans. Because of the strange motion, up and down and side to side, neither of them could face the food that Melony, the dormouse, had hidden beneath the straw. Of course, Melony had no idea how Devonia came to be sleeping by her side; even so, she felt, like all the other animals, a strange desire to care for her and this she did to the best of her ability.

On the days when the rocking motion was at its least, they drank the fluid from the egg which Melony had stored in her little nutshells and they feasted on the meagre store which the clever dormouse had set aside for the winter.

All this time, faithful Jacko sat up above, at the very top of the ship, obeying his Master's last command. Where do you think he slept? Of course, you are right. It was the Crow's Nest. So all in all everyone did not fare too badly.

Day after day, week after week, the little ship pressed on towards its destiny. One afternoon, after many months as sea, a great commotion was heard by Devonia and Melony and from high above a voice cried, "Land Ho!"

For some time now their little prison had seemed to get warmer each day and the thick black substance which blocked the entrance had become very sticky indeed. Suddenly, Devonia and her companion realised that the terrible rocking motion, which they had endured for so long, had almost ceased and outside they could hear great excitement. It was at this moment that a blinding light suddenly burst upon them as a large portion of the black tar fell away at the top of the hole. Devonia was overjoyed to see the marvellous sunlight and rushed to the top to look out. Melony screamed a warning but, alas! Too late! A second blob of falling tar caught the tip of Devonia's wing and in a split second she was tumbling through the air, her remaining wing flapping uselessly against the weight of the tar. Helplessly she spiralled down and down towards the sea, her pitiful screams drowned by the voices of the humans.

But even fate was to be sympathetic towards the little princess for, with a little 'plop', she landed as lightly as a feather on the top of a lovely soft coonskin cap which was worn by one of the trappers who had come out in boats to ferry the new arrivals ashore. The old trapper cast his eyes aloft and muttered a curse on all seagulls, completely unaware of the presence of his little passenger.

Up above Melony rushed to the edge of the hole and peered down towards the water. Large tears began to trickle down her face as she realised that her friend, who had shared such discomfort with her, had gone forever. A great guilt crept over her; slowly she crawled back to the darkest corner of the hole and cried herself to sleep.

Jacko, who had already searched everywhere for little Devonia, had a very keen sense of hearing and even above all the clanking and shouting heard Devonia's terrified screams. In a flash, he swooped down to the bottom of the ship just in time to see her enclosed by the fur. In grim determination he settled on the prow of the trapper's boat so that he would not be parted from his little ward.

Very soon the boats were on their way to the shore and the passengers cast a wary eye on this strange land that was to be their new home. Devonia tugged and pulled with all her might to free herself from the sticky tar that held her firmly to the fur of the trapper's hat.

As you may know, fairies grow up faster than humans but for how long they live nobody seems to know. Even during the voyage Devonia had grown considerably and had become a lovely young princess. Although she had not yet flown, she had experienced the strange feeling of weightlessness as she exercised her wings during the voyage.

Meanwhile, wicked Witch Hazel was in dire straits. She had never been to sea before and had completely underestimated the size of the ocean; she had no water or food with her at all. A day or two after the voyage began, she had tried to land on the ship but people on deck had seen her and, although some fled in terror, others beat her off with sticks and boat oars. She couldn't turn back because she didn't know the way home and neither did her magic broomstick for that matter. For weeks on end Witch Hazel lived on flying fish and rainwater that she caught in her hat and by this time she had stopped her cackling altogether.

The weeks passed. One day, half asleep and half starved, Witch Hazel crashed into the topmost sails of the ship and there she stayed in terror lest people below should see her. There she lay, sound asleep, as the boat carrying our little friend Devonia reached the shore.

Of course, we must not forget old Kitwillie. Alas! The two tireless dolphins had taken on an impossible task and, over the weeks, had fallen further and further behind. Kitwillie, being a kindly old soul, finally drew them to a halt and set them free so that they may feed and rest awhile. Before they swam away, they said that they would return next day and, sure enough, early next morning they slipped into their harness and were again on their way. By now, they had completely lost sight of the ship. Kitwillie began to feel increasingly alarmed.

Suddenly, one of the dolphin's uttered a very strange sound and after a few seconds a reply came back faintly through the murky waters. The two dolphins immediately changed course and headed in the direction of the friendly whale who had answered them, saying that the ship had passed him a few hours previously.

After all the hard rowing back and forth, the trapper returned to his cabin some miles distant, plonked himself down outside on an old chair and threw his hat onto a nearby rock.

Poor Devonia didn't know what was happening. One second she was flying through the air and the next – crash! The hat struck the rock. Devonia shot forward and her wing was torn free from the sticky tar.

Before she could even open her wings, she hit the ground with a thud. She opened her eyes; at the same time she heard the sound that had sent chills down the spine of many a strong man. There, not more than six inches in front of her was the most loathsome thing that Devonia had ever seen : a monster with hatred in its eyes that froze her little body right through.

Slowly, the monster's terrible head moved back and our little princess sensed that her end was nigh; with the speed of lightning it flew forwards. Devonia shut her eyes in terror and did not see Jacko as he struck like a Black Thunderbolt from the sky. He struck the wicked head as it moved forward, gouging with beak and talons for all he was worth.

Rattly had never experienced such treatment and before he realised what was happening Jacko had plucked Devonia off the rock and was soaring up into the sky to safety.

The poor fairy was almost as terrified by this new threat as she had been by the rattlesnake but, as soon as she looked into Jacko's eyes, she knew she was safe; she was already beginning to acquire the great power of all fairies.

h! What terror! Jacko was trembling from beak to tail. He could not believe that he'd been so brave. Still in a state of shock he flew blindly on. Slowly his fear grew less and, finally, he came to rest on a branch and gently placed Devonia beside him. He then began to tell her of his kind old Master, the hazards of the voyage and the evils of Witch Hazel who had been her mother's worst enemy. He continued by telling her of the great secret, of how he had been locked in a cage by Witch Hazel and how he had been rescued by his wonderful Master. He begged her to keep his secret because old Kitwillie knew nothing of his life before his imprisonment in that dreadful cage and he did not wish to sadden the old man.

Blink! Blink! Hazel's eyes opened and she couldn't believe what she saw: land, beautiful land, everywhere. She suddenly remembered why she was there. "The fairy! Where's the fairy?" she screamed at the poor old broomstick.

He didn't answer. Magic or not, he didn't like her screaming at him. He began to think in his magical way of the lovely serene days spent in old Kitwillie's castle and, because his twigs were from a weeping willow tree, a little moisture seeped from a crack in the wood of his body. "Find the fairy", she screamed, giving him a whack against the mast of the ship; dutifully, he obeyed by flying Witch Hazel towards the spot where Jacko and Devonia rested.

Jacko and Witch Hazel saw each other at the same moment but before Jacko could croak a warning the old hag was upon them, her old gnarled hand grabbing for Devonia. More in fright than intention, the little fairy's wings hummed and, for the first time in her short life, she was flying under her own power.

Round and round the tree, in and out the branches, she flew, Witch Hazel only inches behind her. She looked behind her and in her terror made a dreadful mistake by flying headlong into a very large pinecone.

Down! Down she plunged, almost senseless, completely out of control.

naware of all the fuss up above, Chief Running Deer was sitting outside his tepee in the shade of a big pine tree, enjoying a doze and sucking gently on his peace pipe which, luckily for our little falling bundle, had gone out.

Plop! Devonia dropped right into the bowl of Running Deer's pipe almost breaking his two front teeth. His eyes flew open; nearly popped out. Never in all his life had he seen anything like this. Before he could gather his wits, old Witch Hazel flew straight across the clearing in front of him. This was too much for the old chief; that's how he got his name: he was last seen running for dear life, never to be heard of again.

His cry was so loud that Witch Hazel nearly fell off her broomstick; she flew into a thicket to hide.

Jacko dived to help Devonia who was still dazed. Soon, she was able to fly again and Jacko suggested that they should try to find their way back to the ship in the hope that his Master would come one day. No matter which way they flew, they only succeeded in losing themselves deep in this vast wilderness.

Days turned to weeks and weeks to months and slowly they realised that they would never see their homeland again.

The old Witch was always close behind and, on several occasions, Jacko saved the little princess from her clutches. Once, he pecked her nose so hard that she fell from her broomstick in mid air and only a marvellous piece of aerobatics by her broomstick saved her from certain disaster. Afterwards, the broomstick wondered why he bothered and, of course, even after saving her, she beat him for letting her fall off in the first place.

Gradually the months turned to years. Devonia grew into a beautiful princess, her powers becoming greater all the time enabling her to outwit wicked old Hazel.

One day, whilst they rested by an old barn, on one of the settlers' homesteads, they heard the sound of weeping. Devonia peered round an old wicker basket and saw a sad little dormouse, head in hands. The dormouse looked up. Devonia looked down. Suddenly, they were in each other's arms, laughing and crying at the same time for it was none other than her friend Melony who had cared for her during the terrible voyage. Devonia was so overjoyed that she grasped Melony by the hands and danced round and round in the grass. It was some time before Jacko understood their antics but, when he did, he tried to join in the fun. Melony said how sad she had been because the animals blamed her for not looking after Devonia properly.

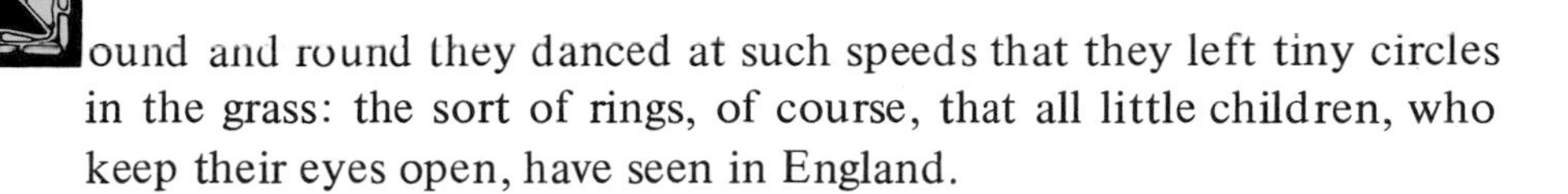

Round and round they danced at such speeds that they left tiny circles in the grass: the sort of rings, of course, that all little children, who keep their eyes open, have seen in England.

Just then, the little boy and girl who lived in the settler's cabin, appeared from behind the hedge in the garden. The little girl, with eyes open wide, spotted the fairy rings immediately.
"Oh! Look!", she cried. "Fairy Rings!"
"Poppycock", said her brother, "no such things as fairies".

The world stopped dead. Every single animal, every single bird, and every single fish stopped in their tracks. For one split second it seemed as if there was no sound on earth.

Happy Devonia was half a jump in the air when the boy said the fatal words. It was as if she had been struck by an arrow. She collapsed in a tiny pile on the grass. For a moment, Jacko was struck totally dumb. Melony couldn't move at all. Recovering themselves a little, they gently carried the little princess into the barn and laid her on an old lambskin. No matter what they did Devonia could not be awakened.

Day and night, Melony bathed Devonia's forehead and never left her side. On the fourth day, Melony looked into Jacko's eyes and they both realised the terrible truth. The very next day, the little fairy's breathing was so faint that they knew the end was near. Poor Jacko could not bear to stand there any longer. He flew onto the roof and croaked at the top of his voice to the whole world, hoping that someone would help.

Alas! No one could. The damage was irreversible.
Wicked Witch Hazel peered out through the straw where she was hiding, cackled and rubbed her old hands with glee. Despite all her power, it had taken a misguided little boy to do what she had failed to achieve.

here was one very old man who *did* hear Jacko's lamented cry and, tired and old as he was after years of heartbreaking search, he practically broke into a run when he heard it.

Yes! Old Kitwillie had reached the end of his quest. As he rushed into the garden, he almost fell over the handle of the old waterpump and Jacko nearly fell down the chimney in a cloud of feathers when he saw him. He was so overjoyed at the sight of his beloved Master that the old man did not realise that anything was amiss.

"Where is she?" he gently asked, when Jacko had calmed down. Jacko was too overcome to reply; instead, he led Kitwillie into the barn where Devonia lay. The old man dropped to his knees and immediately recognised the symptoms. He had seen them many times before. There was nothing he could do. He gently lifted the tiny creature from her bed and, as he did so, her little eyes fluttered open and a beautiful smile flickered across her face; her tiny arms reached out and Devonia passed away.

As you may know, Wizards never cry and old Kitwillie, who had travelled so far for so many years, was no exception but, without the power of his magic wand, he was almost reduced to the standards of a normal human; slowly but surely a tiny tear began to form and then another and another until he could contain himself no longer and tears coursed down his face.

A Wizard's teardrops? This was something unheard of; something so rare it must be of the highest magical order. Teardrops fell all over Devonia's limp form and splashed everywhere. Jacko, who was also crying, was thoroughly soaked by the old man's teardrops.

Then something strange began to take place. Jacko began to change. Slowly but surely the feathers began to fall away; at the same time his form was changing. Within a few seconds, there stood before the old man a handsome Elfin Prince: the very one Witch Hazel had turned into a black jackdaw and locked in her cage, all those years ago.

As Kitwillie stared in amazement, he realised that something else was happening. In his hand, the little fairy was changing colour; a faint yellow tint came into her skin, growing brighter every second.

The yellow turned to a dazzling hue,
Kitwillie realised his wish had come true.
His one last wish and his great endeavour
Was that this last fairy may last forever.
He had endured so much to fulfil his dream,
He owed that much to her mother, the Queen.
And then, as if from a beautiful mould
Devonia turned into glittering gold.

In his surprise, Kitwillie almost dropped the tiny statue. From its base came a tiny wisp of vapour. Never had he seen such magic! Gradually the mist began to thicken and, to everyone's amazement, began to take on a human form: first the arms, then the legs, then a face appeared; last of all the body and wings.

There before them stood Devonia beside the empty shell. The old man was dumbfounded. He looked at the golden shell. He looked at Devonia, reached out and gingerly touched her, fully expecting her to disappear; instead she smiled, flew up and kissed him on the cheek. Kitwillie began to laugh (perhaps a little hysterically) but laugh he did. Melony, who was rooted to the spot, began to laugh; then the handsome Jack began to laugh and, finally, Devonia, who didn't know what they were laughing at, joined in which seemed to make it all the funnier.

Wicked old Hazel, however, was not laughing. Never had she seen magic of this magnitude. She was so livid that she almost burst. She flew into such a rage that the straw around her suddenly burst into flames; she ran out of the barn in a terrible panic, leaving poor Willow to perish in the fire. The magic broomstick shot out of the flames with his twigs alight and flew straight to Kitwillie who promptly dipped him in the water butt. From that moment, Willow decided never to return to Witch Hazel.

Having put out the fire, the old man reverently laid to rest the golden shell from which Devonia had emerged. He placed it beneath a large old log and received the shock of his life when it suddenly reared up, revealing a large head with snapping teeth.

Yes! It was a crocodile! It frightened them all so much that they jumped onto the magic broomstick and decided to leave this country forever.

Even Kitwillie did not realise the power instilled in his teardrops for, each year, on the anniversary of Devonia's rebirth, a beautiful translucent mist appears, emerging from the golden shell which, to this very day, still remains hidden from the sight of man; therefore, according to our reckoning, there are now some three hundred and and sixty-four of these tiny beings, living happily and managing to cope with the antics of old Witch Hazel.

When Kitwillie, Devonia, Jack and Melony flew over the coast of the New World, they could see old Witch Hazel sitting in a rockpool, soothing her scorched skin, cursing and ranting when she saw them flying above. To our knowledge that is where she is to this very day.

Finally, the tired foursome, who had seen such great adventures, came to that lovely green country they knew so well, landed old Willow (who was also pretty tired by now) right on the lawn of Kitwillie's Castle. There, on his door, was a tiny note surrounded by a garland of withered flowers. It read like this:

We were the ones who found your wand
And hid it well that day;
We have hunted everywhere
But can't recall the way.
Do not worry about your wand,
We shall restore your power.
Meet us in the forest glade
Where grows the magic flower.

Signed: the Fairies

The old man was completely overcome with joy. Devonia wasn't the last fairy after all!

One week later, Devonia and Jack were married in the Wizard's garden and, one by one, the fairies, elves and pixies seemed to appear from nowhere and last, but not least, guess who?

Yes! You are quite right. That naughty little Hobgoblin had escaped from that bubble somehow!

The End

Between the countries of the world
This is a special race,
So people of Great Britain
You really must keep pace.
The fairies hid Kitwillie's wand
In a very secret spot;
The answer lies within the sun
Where it's very, very hot;
When you have found the secret place
You'll see it rises up.
But there are two; what must you do?
Try tea-leaves in a cup?
Collect all the clues
And solve this riddle
Go there to dig
Right in the middle.

Having read the poems and story
And found the clue that's right
Do not delay – go right away
Go you at dead of night;
Stand you in the centre
No stars must be in sight
Then go as far as you may go
But go you to the right.
You are very close my friend
To the second place of birth
But go ye on, but two feet more,
And dig ye in the earth.

ISBN 0 9508999 0 9

First published 1983
First Edition 1983

FRED HANCOCK'S
Original works of
art are exhibited
by Portal Gallery
16A Grafton Street,
Bond Street,
London W.1. England.